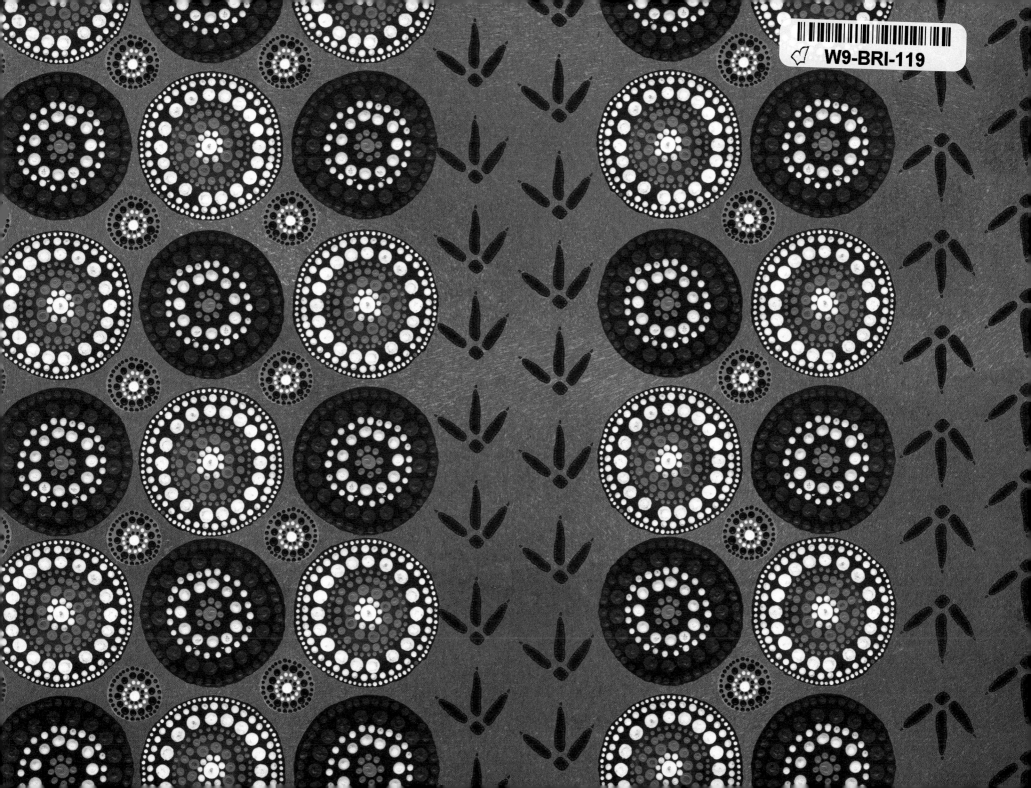

Silly Birds

To my beautiful daughter Biarra,
and my awesome son Korraki.

Always believe in yourself,
and set your dreams and goals high.

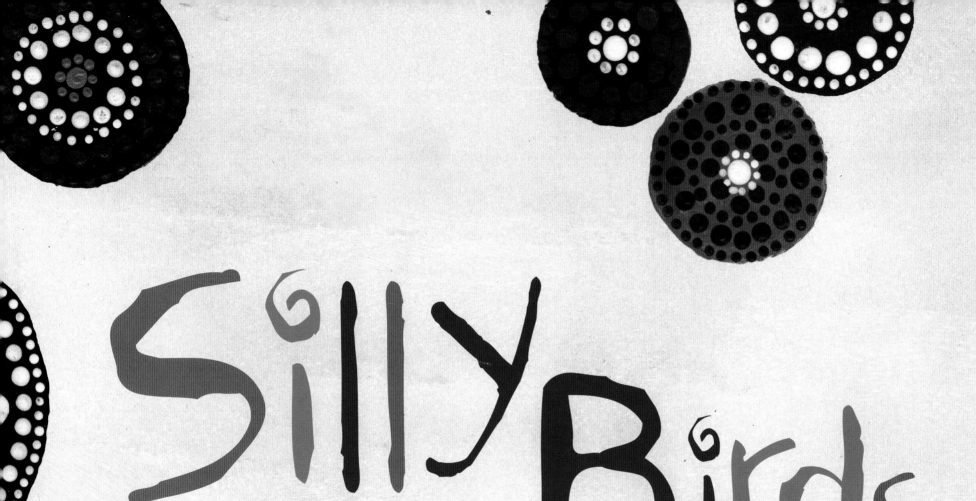

Silly Birds

written and illustrated by

Gregg Dreise

Magabala
Books

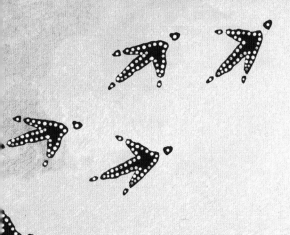

Way back before **Once-upon-a-time** time,
there was the Dreamtime, and during this
period there was Maliyan.

Maliyan was an eagle and his parents were extremely
proud of him. Maliyan was well looked after by his
family and made to feel special.

Maliyan always looked and listened, and rarely spoke. His parents told him that speaking too much was only for the silly birds. He didn't want to be a silly bird. He didn't want to be a wombah thigaraa.

So Maliyan learnt how to listen and how to see things a long way away. As Maliyan got older, he became well respected.

Until he met Wagun.

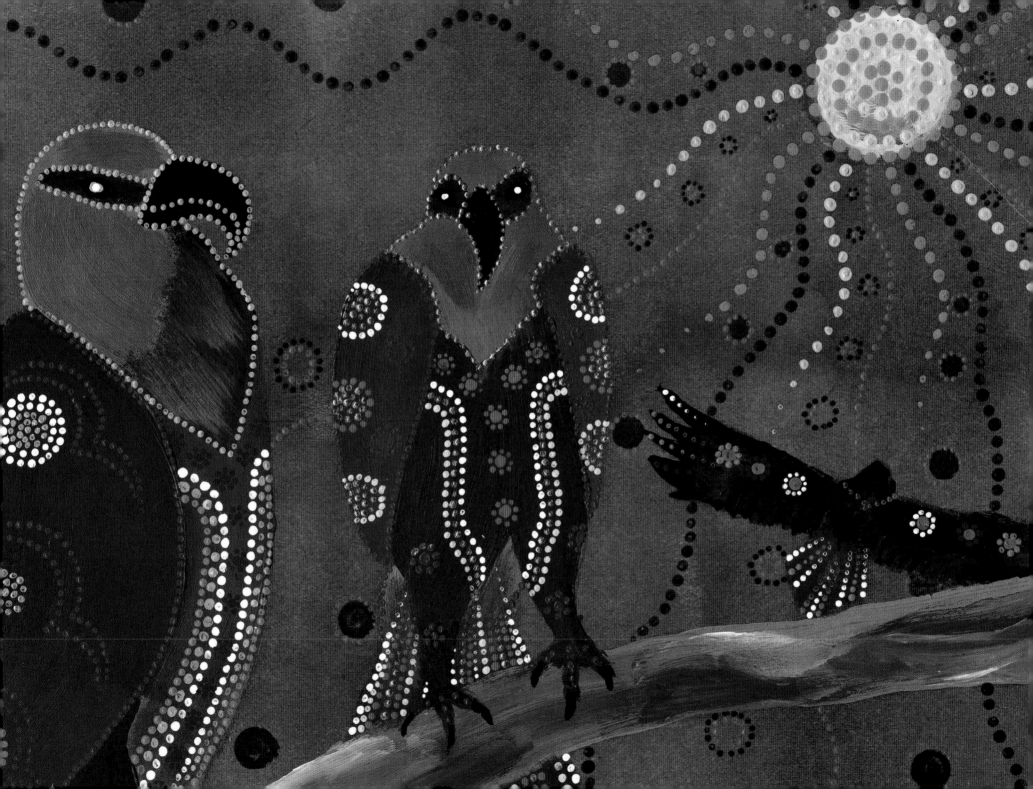

Wagun was a wombah thigaraa, a silly bird. He never looked nor listened. He was always running around knocking things over. Sometimes he even knocked over the Elders, the wise ones.

Wagun was always talking, and usually about himself. He bragged that he was the best. He told everyone, even his parents and the Elders, that he was better than them.

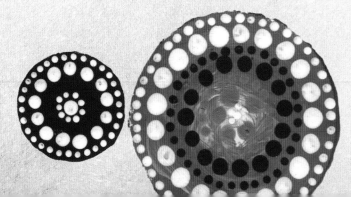

Wagun told the Elders that he was faster than them. Whenever they tried to talk to him, he didn't listen. Instead he would say, "Why do I need to listen to you old birds? I am stronger, faster and smarter than you!"

The Elders just shook their heads. Many tried to talk to him, but he didn't listen. Soon, most of the birds gave up on Wagun, but Maliyan didn't.
Maliyan thought he was fun.

Maliyan and Wagun began to sing together. They didn't sing the old songs the Elders had taught them, but new songs they made up themselves – silly songs that poked fun at others. They even made up silly dances to go with the silly songs.

All too soon, Maliyan began to follow Wagun everywhere. All too soon, Maliyan forgot to look and listen and, just like Wagun, he started to talk too much.

The Elders grew concerned. Other young birds joined Maliyan and Wagun. Soon there were lots of silly birds. With lots of wombah thigaraas, things that always went right began to go wrong.

The wombah thigaraas began to throw their rubbish into the billabong. Before long the water became too polluted to drink. The silly birds began to eat too much food. Food became harder and harder to find.

Maliyan's once proud parents lost sleep. The pride they had in their son began to shrink each night with the setting sun. They shook their worried heads at him, and Maliyan began to feel bad.

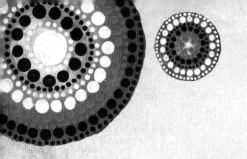

Maliyan's heart ached. His kind heart knew he had to make a change. Maliyan flew to the Elders for advice, and they were glad to help. They kept saying to Maliyan, "It is hard to soar like an eagle, when you are surrounded by turkeys."

Soon Maliyan began to understand. Maliyan tried to tell Wagun and the others, but they were too busy talking to listen to him.

Maliyan remembered that he didn't need to talk. His power was in his ability to see and hear things from a long way away. Maliyan's power was in his ability to look and listen.

Soon Maliyan grew in strength. He became a wonderful hunter and a wise leader. He passed on the wisdom of the Elders to the younger birds and, luckily, they listened to him.

Maliyan was once again a proud eagle.

The birds looked and listened and cleaned up their billabong. They practised their old songs and dances and looked after their country. Together, they worked to build for the future.

All except Wagun.

Wagun lost his ability to fly high. He became selfish and continued to try to have fun. He didn't realise he was lonely and had no friends. He still scratched around in his own world.

Today, all turkeys scratch around on the ground trying to find seeds, small plants and fallen berries. They can fly, but not very well.

Now, the eagles remind their children about the story of Maliyan.

Children are reminded to always look and listen before speaking.

To always respect Elders' knowledge and experience.

To only take what you need and never be too greedy.

And to always choose your friends wisely, because it is hard to soar like an eagle when you are surrounded by turkeys.

Thanks

To my wonderful mother, for your poems and competitions, I love you.

To my talented father, I love your support and your artwork too.

To all my family, having your support and laughter always warms my heart.

To Uncle Reg Knox, thank you for your time, wisdom, stories and art.

To the Elders, I thank you and cherish all you have been through.

To our future generations, there is still so much for us to do.

Always be proud of yourself and your culture, never forget who you are.

Always learn about family and tradition, as they will take you far.

Gregg Dreise

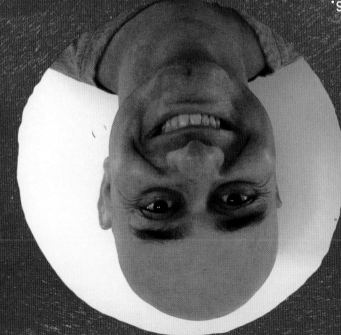

Gregg Dreise is a descendant of the Kamilaroi tribe, from south-west Queensland and north-west New South Wales. Gregg was born and raised in St George, Queensland and has seven older brothers and sisters. All his brothers were good at running and footy and his sisters were good at netball. Gregg was lucky to have been raised in a family that loved sport, music and poetry.

Gregg's mother (Lyla Dreise-Knox) has always inspired him to write. Her poetry has entertained the family (as well as the odd magazine and newspaper reader) for many decades.

Gregg is currently a teacher on the Sunshine Coast.

The inspiration for this story came from Gregg's uncle, Reg Knox. He told a yarn about how he worked with some Italian farmers who trained a cockatoo to speak English and Italian. Reg Knox often said that if a small-brained bird could do that, then people, especially kids, could learn anything when they put in the effort.

As he was growing up, Gregg often heard the Elders saying that it was 'hard to soar like an eagle when you are surrounded by turkeys'. It took him a while to truly understand what they were saying.

First published 2014 reprinted 2014
Magabala Books Aboriginal Corporation
Broome, Western Australia, 6725
Website: www.magabala.com Email: sales@magabala.com

Magabala Books receives financial assistance from the
Commonwealth Government through the Australia Council,
its arts advisory body. The State of Western Australia has
made an investment in this project through the Department
of Culture and the Arts in association with Lotterywest.

Designed by Tracey Gibbs
Printed in China by 1010 Printing International Limited

National Library of Australia
Cataloguing–in–Publication entry

Dreise, Gregg, author, illustrator.
Silly birds/Gregg Dreise, author and illustrator.

9781922142993

For primary school age.

Dreamtime (Aboriginal Australian mythology)--Juvenile
fiction.
Listening--Juvenile fiction.
Birds--Juvenile fiction.

Dewey Number: A823.4

The term 'wombah thigaraa' or
silly birds comes from the
Gamilaraay language as spoken by the
Kamilaroi peoples of south-western
Queensland and north-western
New South Wales.